SUPER BOWL
SWITCH
I Was Dan Marino

GORDON KORMAN

HYPERION PAPERBACKS FOR CHILDREN
NEW YORK

SPECIAL EDITION

Printed in the United States of America.

This book is set in 12-point Caslon.

Library of Congress Catalog Card Number: 97-71799
ISBN: 0-7868-4243-1

Contents

The Saliva Blitz Pocket Fire Pass

The NFL Monday Night Football Club gathered around the doghouse. Inside, Lady Godiva, the friendliest dog in Middletown, snored softly. One floppy Saint Bernard ear stirred up and down with each noisy breath. Her long glistening tongue lolled out of her slack mouth. Lady Godiva was worthy of her nickname—Lady Saliva.

"Look at that," murmured Nick Lighter. "Even in her sleep she drools."

"Couldn't we do this trick play without her?" complained Coleman Galloway.

"Don't be stupid," said Elliot Rifkin, the third member of the group. "How could we have the Saliva Blitz Pocket Fire Pass without Lady Saliva?"

"Listen, Coleman," Nick assured. "Lady Saliva won't hurt you. She loves everybody. When she wakes up and sees you standing there, she's going to run at you and start licking."

"I know," shuddered Coleman. "It's disgusting!"

"She's the blitz," Elliot explained. "As quarterback, it's your job to fire-pass the ball to Nick before Lady Saliva sacks you. And I'm on defense covering Nick. Okay, let's go."

Coleman's voice was shaky as he called, "Hut, hut, *hike*!"

The play unfolded smoothly. Elliot snapped the ball to Coleman. Then he and Nick began pounding on the roof of the doghouse. At the first "Woof!" they both took off downfield, out of range. When Lady Godiva burst out into the open, the one and only target for her love and affection was Coleman.

"Throw!" chorused Nick and Elliot.

But Coleman lost his nerve. As Lady Godiva bounded toward him in a shower of dog drool, all he could think of was escape.

He tucked the ball under his arm and ran, yelling all the way, "He-e-e-elp!"

He made it five yards. The big Saint Bernard flattened him like a steamroller and held him there, pinned, to be licked and adored.

Nick was ready with the dog biscuit. He rushed up, waved the treat under Lady Godiva's nose, and hurled it as far as he could across the lawn.

If there was anything Lady Godiva loved more than people, it was food. She abandoned Coleman and went after the snack.

Nick held an imaginary microphone in front of Coleman's wet face. "Tell the folks at home: how does it feel to be sacked by a dog?" It was the postgame interview that followed all their trick plays.

Coleman was trying to dry his hair with the sleeve of his jacket. "Sacked? I was almost drowned! Next time we try the Saliva Blitz Pocket Fire Pass, I want to wear a raincoat."

"And now a word from our sponsor," Nick persisted.

"Aw, I'm not in the mood," Coleman grumbled.

"You know the rules," Elliot reminded him. "All Monday Night Football Club trick plays have to have commercials."

"I've got one," put in Nick. "Check it out: 'Don't let this happen to you. Coleman Galloway didn't drink his Mega-Mega-Muscle-Ade, and he messed up the Saliva Blitz Pocket Fire Pass. As a penalty, he has to be the odd man out on the field trip.'"

The fifth-graders were going on a two-day visit to New York City next week. The principal had decided that the students would travel on the buddy system, in pairs. The Monday Night Football Club had protested, complained, requested, and finally begged to be allowed to form a group of three. No dice.

So the Saliva Blitz Pocket Fire Pass was the test. Whoever flubbed the trick play was out. Coleman had to find himself another buddy.

"I'm not going," Coleman growled. "I'll tell my mom I've got Dutch elm disease."

Elliot laughed. "Only trees get that."

"Well, I'll think of something else, then. I'm sure there must be plenty of terrible germs you can get from dog drool."

"What are you—nuts, Coleman?" Nick demanded. "Of course you have to come to New York! It's Super Bowl Sunday!"

That was the craziest part of it all. Out of 365 possible squares on the calendar, the travel day was booked for Super Bowl Sunday.

Super Bowl Sunday! The day the Monday Night Football Club waited for all year! The icing on the cake of the football season! Why, the entire world shut down on Super Bowl Sunday! People planned parties, visited relatives, held open houses, enjoyed a festive atmosphere—almost a national holiday. One thing they did not do was board a bus bound for New York City so they could miss the world championship game.

Each member of the Monday Night Football Club

presented his parents with a list of the things that would happen long before he would ever miss the Super Bowl:

    1. Water buffalo would learn to tap-dance

    2. Chocolate would be declared health food

    3. It would snow on the Fourth of July in Puerto Rico

    4. The Supreme Court would repeal the law of gravity

    5. I would eat my own foot

The fifth grade parents supported the school. But there were questions—mainly, "What genius picked this date?"

Embarrassed, the principal tried to make everybody happy. The bus would depart early. The museum tour would end in plenty of time. The students would be settled in the YMCA's TV lounge. No one would have to miss the Super Bowl.

The Monday Night Football Club still wasn't happy. They were used to their weekly sleep-overs to watch Monday Night Football. To them, the Super Bowl was Monday night times fifty.

"It stinks," was Coleman's opinion. "We have our own way of doing things—pizza, sleeping bags, privacy. It won't be the same in some YMCA with the whole fifth grade."

Nick sighed. "You heard our folks. We watch the game in New York, or not at all."

"What do you care, Coleman?" added Elliot. "You're not even going to be there, really. The Super Bowl is your day—last chance this season to try out the sweater."

The sweater was an old moth-eaten football jersey once worn by Nick's grandfather, who had played college football for the North Brainerd Eskimos. There was one very remarkable secret about it. Anyone who fell asleep wearing it would somehow be transported into the body of a famous football star. No one quite understood why it happened, but no one questioned it, either. The opportunity to play in an NFL game was far too amazing to pass up. Nick and Elliot claimed it was the greatest thrill in the world. Now it was Coleman's turn.

"I—I'm not so sure that's a good idea," Coleman stammered. "After all, we'll be away from home, in a strange city—"

"This is the Super Bowl!" Nick interrupted. "The championship!"

"You're wimping out again, aren't you?" accused Elliot.

Coleman was offended. "I never wimped out!"

"Of course not," Nick said sarcastically. "Let's see: once you had a rash and the shirt was too itchy; once you were sniffling—you didn't want to give your cold to any of the Chicago Bears; the ingrown toenail held you back for a couple of Mondays; and last week there was that history test, and you were afraid all your studying would get left in the mind of some San Francisco 49er."

"I promise. I'll really do it this time," vowed Coleman.

"Then you'd better find a buddy for the trip," Nick urged. "You don't want to get stuck with a loser like Matthew Leopold."

"But you guys are the only people I like!"

Elliot's eyes gleamed. "I know. Why don't you ask Caitlin Mooney? You've been working up the courage to talk to her for three years."

"That's not true!" raged Coleman. Then, in a lower voice he said, "She doesn't have a partner yet?"

"I saw the buddy list," Elliot confirmed. "She's not on it."

The Biggest Chicken in Town

Caitlin Mooney was the most popular girl in the fifth grade. Her long dark hair and brown eyes gave Coleman chills. Gazing at her across the playground after school the next day scared him to death.

How would he ever get up the guts to ask her? "She's so somebody, and I'm so nobody," he mumbled to himself. What could he say? He had to plan it out, get the words exactly right—

"Hey, Caitlin!" bellowed Nick. "Get over here! Coleman has to talk to you!"

Horrified, Coleman elbowed his friend so hard that Nick went flying into the hedge that surrounded the portables. "Shut up!" Coleman hissed.

By the time he turned back to the school yard, Caitlin was standing in front of him.

"Uh—uh—hi," he managed.

"Hi." She smiled, which made things worse. "What's up?"

"Well—," Coleman forgot his carefully planned speech because Elliot had positioned himself behind Caitlin. He was making faces.

"Go away!" Coleman snarled. "No! Not you, Caitlin. Uh—the thing is—like—do you want to be my buddy for the field trip on Sunday?"

She looked uncomfortable. "I'm sorry, Coleman. But the New York trip is the most exciting thing we've ever done at this school. Face it, when do we get to go somewhere cool? It could be a real adventure. And—well, no offense—but everyone knows you're the biggest chicken in town. You can't have an adventure with a chicken."

Nick burst out of the bushes, bristling with outrage. "Let me tell you something, Caitlin. In your wildest dreams you could never imagine the kind of adventure this guy is going to have in New York!"

"Yeah!" roared Elliot from behind her. "He's no chicken! If you go to the dictionary and look up *adventure*, you'll find a picture of Coleman!" He threw an arm around his friend's shoulder. "Come on, man. Forget Caitlin. Let's go bungee jumping."

"And skydiving," Nick tossed over his shoulder as the three walked away.

"And alligator wrestling," added Elliot.

"Don't forget being shot out of a cannon," Nick called back.

But Caitlin had already melted into the crowd on the playground.

Coleman was impressed. "Gee, guys, did you really mean all that stuff about me being in the dictionary?"

"What do you think?" growled Elliot. "Of course you're a chicken. You do everything but lay eggs."

"But she's got a lot of nerve insulting a Monday Night Football Club member," added Nick. "We couldn't let her get away with it."

"Am I really such a wimp?" Coleman asked dejectedly as he trudged along.

"Get real!" Nick exclaimed. "You gave away your football cards after the first paper cut! You have nightmares about your mom's eyebrow tweezers! You're even scared to play in the Super Bowl—the chance of a lifetime!"

"But I'm going to do it," Coleman vowed stoutly. "Maybe I'll get to be a quarterback. They don't have to hit people."

Elliot stared at him. "Are you nuts? Quarterbacks have to be the toughest guys in the NFL. They have to stand in the pocket and pass while bone-crushing linebackers come roaring down on them! *You* couldn't get off a throw because you were afraid of getting licked by Lady Saliva!"

"Like that's the same thing!" scoffed Coleman. "I can just picture a superstar like Dan Marino having to take a spit bath from some mutt!"

"He takes a lot worse than that every game," Nick pointed out. "Quarterbacks have to be fearless."

"What for?" Coleman shrugged. "They've got a wall of three-hundred-pound linemen protecting them."

They turned up the Galloways' front walk, and Coleman let them into the house.

"Anyway, you're no Dan Marino," Nick was saying. "You've had the Eskimos sweater in your closet for over a month. And I'll bet money you haven't even had the guts to try it on and see how it feels."

"You've got that right," confirmed Coleman. "It's itchy!"

Elliot glared at him. "You see what we're talking about? You're a coward! A jellyfish! A scaredy-cat—"

"Enough!" Coleman exploded. "I'll put on the shirt right now if it'll make you guys happy!" He stormed down the hall to his room and threw open the closet door.

The old brown sweater was not there.

"Mo-o-o-om!!"

Nick was panic-stricken. "Maybe you put it in a drawer!"

"No! It was there! Right on my lucky hanger!"

Mrs. Galloway burst into the room. "For goodness' sake, Coleman. I thought someone was being murdered in here!"

"Where's the shirt?" Coleman cried. "The brown football sweater with the orange number thirteen?"

His mother frowned. "You mean that moth-eaten old thing on your lucky hanger?"

"The Eskimos sweater!" breathed Elliot, nodding himself dizzy.

She looked surprised. "What's the big fuss? Surely you weren't planning to *wear* it anywhere, Coleman. I wouldn't allow you to step out the front door in that thing. It was a rag!"

"*Was?*" Coleman wheezed. "Don't say *was*! Say *is*! You didn't throw it out, right?"

"Of course not."

They all sighed with relief.

"I gave it to the Charity Secondhand Shop," Mrs. Galloway finished. "They resell old clothes."

Nick was positive that he had stopped breathing. The shirt! The magic shirt that had allowed him to play a *Monday Night Football* game as John Elway, that had turned Elliot into Barry Sanders—the most fabulous item that any of them would see in their lifetimes was missing! *And just before Super Bowl Sunday!*

There was a moment of perfect, silent agony. Then the Monday Night Football Club turned like a marching band and sprinted out of the house.

Elliot did the talking.

"We're looking for a football sweater," he gasped, still panting from the ten-block run to the Charity Secondhand Shop. "Maybe something in brown, with an orange number—thirteen would be good." He added, "Do you happen to have anything like that?"

The store clerk smiled sympathetically. "Oh, poor you. Your mom gave away your favorite shirt, didn't she?"

Coleman spoke up. "No, it was *my* mom."

"And it was *my* shirt," finished Nick. "It's here, right?"

"Not exactly," the woman admitted. "We felt it was too"—she paused—"well-worn to sell."

"Are you kidding?" cried Nick. "That shirt is priceless! You could get a million bucks for it! Easy!"

"But we're prepared to offer"—they had a quick conference—"six dollars and eighteen cents," put in Elliot.

"You don't understand," the woman explained. "I

don't have it anymore. But feel free to look for it in the trash out back."

She moved to open the counter door. But they were already up and over and running into the alley behind the store.

"Wait a minute!" exclaimed Coleman. "These garbage cans are all empty!"

Three pairs of horrified eyes flew to the entrance of the small lane. A Middletown sanitation truck was just turning out into the street.

"*Sto-o-op!*" came a heartrending chorus from the Monday Night Football Club.

They took off like football wedge-busters covering a punt return. Coleman, the fastest, pulled ahead. He tore out of the alley with Nick and Elliot in hot pursuit.

The garbage truck was halted at a red light. Coleman's eyes bulged. Hanging out of the back of the hopper was a familiar brown sleeve. It blew in the breeze as if it was waving good-bye to them. He caught up and stood there, panting.

Nick came up behind him. "What are you waiting for? Pull it out!"

Coleman hesitated. "Do you think we have to ask permission?"

Nick grabbed the sleeve and started yanking. "You

can't steal from a garbage truck! It's *garbage!*"

The light turned green, and the big truck shifted gears with a grinding sound.

Coleman and Elliot clamped their hands onto the brown scratchy wool. This was their last chance. If the truck got up to speed, the next stop would be the Middletown dump and incinerator, five miles outside the city limits.

The truck lurched forward, and the Monday Night Football Club gave one desperate heave-ho. The Eskimos sweater popped out of the hopper, sending its three rescuers flying backward. They picked themselves and their treasure up off the road and scrambled to the safety of the sidewalk.

"That was a close one!" gasped Elliot, brushing eggshells off the brown shirt.

Nick inspected his grandfather's college uniform. "Phew! It's good as new—you know, for a fifty-year-old sweater." He buried his face in it. "It didn't even pick up any garbage smells." He looked daggers at Coleman. "No thanks to you!"

"Blame my mother, not me!" Coleman defended himself. "And there's a bigger problem. I can take this home and hide it, but she's never going to let me pack it for New York."

"How you get it to New York is *your* business, Coleman," insisted Elliot. "But it had better be there."

"What if it's impossible?" Coleman whined.

"You *make* it possible," ordered Nick, deadly serious. "The shirt is a part of the Monday Night Football Club. And if *you* want to stay a part of the club, you'll have it for the Super Bowl."

Coleman gawked in horror. Surely his two best friends would never kick him out of the club! On the other hand, Nick wouldn't joke about a thing like that. Football was his whole life! He even had the initials N. F. L., for Nicholas Farrel Lighter.

"Okay, okay," Coleman said quickly. "I'll find a way."

"Good man," Elliot approved. "Now you'd better get with the program and find a buddy before you wind up stuck with Matthew Leopold."

Red Alert Force-Five Itch Emergency

Coleman Galloway was miserable with a capital *M*. He sat next to his buddy, Matthew Leopold, as the school bus traveled down the interstate toward New York City.

Being partnered with the biggest creep in the fifth grade was only a small part of his misery. The major torture was the Eskimos jersey. It was on him, because that was the only way he could get it out of the house. Worse, he was wearing it under one of his own sweaters to cover it up—so it was an *undershirt*. The fuzzy scratchy wool against his bare skin was driving him crazy.

This thing was the world's itchiest sweater with ten turtlenecks underneath! Right on his skin, it was like wearing lava! He wouldn't make it to New York! He'd die!

"Mr. Sargent! Mrs. Montrose!" tattled Matthew. "Coleman won't sit still!"

Coleman pressed up against the window and froze himself into a statue. It took as much effort as lifting a piano. With his own clothing (boys' size 12) squeezing the Eskimos sweater (men's XXL), he felt like he was in a sauna being crushed to death by a boa constrictor while fire ants nibbled at his flesh.

He caught sight of Caitlin Mooney. She was looking at him with a frown of disapproval. Uh-oh. Giving in to Matthew was just another proof that Coleman was a wimp and a chicken.

He looked longingly toward the front of the bus. A few rows ahead, Nick and Elliot sat together. He was so jealous he could have died. He knew that they were watching the Super Bowl pregame coverage on Nick's handheld portable TV. He longed to be up there with them. He longed to be anywhere Matthew wasn't.

Coleman couldn't blame the guys for having a good time. They had no way of knowing that their poor friend had the Eskimos sweater under his clothes—and his entire upper body was in a state of Red Alert Force-Five Itch Emergency!

Nick turned to the back of the bus. "How's it going, Coleman?" he called.

Coleman cast him a glare of such total suffering that Nick had to look away.

"Whoa," he told Elliot. "Our friend isn't too happy back there. I think he's swallowed his own lips."

Elliot shrugged. "We warned him to get himself a decent partner."

"He's probably just nervous about trying out the shirt tonight," Nick commented. "I was scared to death when I suddenly woke up on the thirty yard line of Mile High Stadium with a football flying at my face."

"He's the luckiest guy on the face of the earth," said Elliot with certainty. "This is the Super Bowl. Green Bay versus Miami! Do you know how many stars there are on those two teams? And he's going to switch places with one of them!" He focused on the tiny screen. "I hope you brought some extra batteries."

"Are you kidding?" said Nick. "I had a nightmare that the bus broke down, and we had to watch the game here. I've got so many batteries that I didn't have room to pack any underwear!"

Matthew tattled on Coleman every ten minutes of the four-hour ride.

"Mr. Sargent! Mrs. Montrose! Coleman's on my half of the seat!"

"Mr. Sargent! Mrs. Montrose! Coleman's hogging the window!"

"Mr. Sargent! Mrs. Montrose! Coleman's breathing too loud!"

Neither of the teachers so much as turned around.

Matthew's tattling was notorious at Middletown Elementary School. He would not have received any attention even if he'd been screaming that the bus was on fire.

Coleman yawned. What a jerk that Matthew was. "Coleman did this!" "Coleman did that!" His tattling was as regular as the endless parade of telephone poles along the side of the road. He tuned Matthew out and concentrated on the poles, whizzing by, one by one, never ending. . . . His eyelids drooped.

For the first time all day, Coleman smiled. He always fell asleep on long drives, and today it was finally going to pay off. The more he could sleep, the less time he would have to spend listening to Matthew and suffering the mega-itch. He wriggled into a comfortable position and closed his eyes. . . .

Wait a minute! You can't fall asleep! You're wearing the sweater!

Sleep was what triggered the Eskimos shirt! You dozed off, and when you woke up, you were somebody else. But it wasn't time yet! The Super Bowl didn't start till six. It wasn't even noon.

He tried to fight off his drowsiness. It was no use. He had been a car sleeper since he was a baby. Plus he'd been up all last night worrying over how to smuggle the jersey out of the house. He was exhausted. He had to do something drastic to stay awake.

"Hey, Matthew, want to play tic-tac-toe? Or hang-man? Got a deck of cards?"

"I'm not talking to you, Coleslaw," sneered Matthew. "You're the worst buddy on the whole bus."

"But I have to stay awake!" Coleman mumbled to himself. He couldn't keep his eyes open! The telephone poles were blurring together! Oh no! He wasn't ready-y-y-y. . . .

A tiny glowing football appeared just off the end of Coleman's nose. It was the signal that the Eskimos jersey was in operation. The small light—just about the size of a lima bean—began to move in front of Coleman's face. It traced the number *13* and then winked out of existence.

Mr. Sargent stood up at the front of the bus. "What was that? Has somebody got a flashlight back there?"

The only reply came from Matthew Leopold. "Mr. Sargent! Mrs. Montrose! Coleman's snoring!"

"He's got the right idea," Mrs. Montrose approved. "You should all try to have a nap and pass the rest of the trip quietly. We have a very exciting couple of days in New York."

Nick nudged Elliot. "I hope our friend doesn't get so much rest that he can't fall asleep tonight when he's wearing the shirt."

4

The Number One Passer in NFL History

The cashier placed the credit card slip on the counter in front of Coleman. "Your total comes to $814.87."

"What?" Coleman was appalled. "What did I buy? A helicopter?"

He recoiled in shock. *That's not my voice! It's too deep!*

The salesgirl pointed to the velvet jewelry box.

Coleman goggled. "Earrings? What am I supposed to do with earrings?"

She frowned. "You said it was a gift for your wife."

"I don't have a wife!" In a daze, he scribbled his name by the *X*. This was crazy! He didn't even have a credit card! Where was he going to get eight hundred bucks? Just a second ago he was on the school bus headed for New York. What was he doing in an expensive jewelry store in the lobby of some fancy hotel?

His eyes fell on the sign above the front desk: THE SAN DIEGO HILTON.

San Diego, *California*?

It all came crashing down on him—the Eskimos shirt, falling asleep on the bus. It had happened! He was an NFL player, here for the Super Bowl! But who?

The girl took one look at the credit card slip and called, "Security!"

A short stocky man in a Hilton uniform rushed in through the glass door. "What seems to be the prob—" His round face broke into a wide grin. "Hey, it's Dan Marino!"

Shocked, Coleman wheeled to stare at himself in the store mirror. It was true! He was Dan Marino! The number one passer in NFL history! It was a pretty awesome promotion for the biggest chicken in Middletown.

"That's what it says on his Visa," the cashier told the man. "But he signed his name Coleman Galloway. He might be using a stolen credit card."

"Oh, you wanted my *real* name," Coleman stammered. "I thought we were allowed to pick any name."

Shut up, Coleman! he ordered himself. *You're only making it worse!*

"Have you been in a cave the last fifteen years?" the security man asked the cashier. "How can you not recognize Dan Marino?"

"I'm not much of a baseball fan," she admitted to Coleman.

"I play football," he managed.

Well, Dan Marino does, he thought with a gulp.

In about six hours the whole world was going to find out if Coleman Galloway could play it, too.

The Middletown school bus pulled up to the Manhattan YMCA. It lurched to a halt with a squeak of old brakes.

"Stick with your buddies," called Mr. Sargent.

Eagerly, the students got off the bus and stood on the sidewalk, gazing up at the tall buildings all around them.

"Mr. Sargent! Mrs. Montrose!" piped Matthew. "Coleman won't wake up!"

When they ignored him, Matthew shook his buddy. "Come on, Coleslaw. We're here."

Dan Marino lurched awake and stared at the eleven-year-old standing over him. "Yeah, sure, kid. I'll sign your autograph book. Got a pen?"

"You're weird," snorted Matthew. "Come on, let's go."

Marino stared out the window. Crowds of people swarmed in all directions. Taxis whizzed down the avenue, cutting each other off. The sounds of the big city echoed through the bus.

"This looks like New York!" the quarterback exclaimed.

"I wonder why," Matthew said sarcastically.

"But the Super Bowl is in San Diego! What happened to my earrings?"

"Mr. Sargent! Mrs. Montrose!" called Matthew. Then again, louder: *"Mr. Sargent! Mrs. Montrose!"* He ran off the bus and all but threw himself into the teachers' arms. "Coleman's scaring me! I think he's gone crazy!"

Marino appeared in the doorway of the bus. What was he doing on a road trip with fifty kids? Sure, all the Dolphins enjoyed spending time with their fan clubs. But not on Super Bowl Sunday! And definitely not three thousand miles away from San Diego!

He reached up to scratch his chin and felt smooth skin where two days of beard growth was supposed to be. Had these kids *shaved* him while he slept? Were they fans or kidnappers?

Suddenly, he realized that the boy reflected in the big round mirror over the door was scratching his chin, too. He was looking at *himself*!

"I'm a little kid!" he blurted.

"You're a little kid in big trouble if you don't get off the bus," Mr. Sargent told him. "Come on, everybody. Line up. We all have to sign in at the front desk."

The students formed two lines, one for the boys' dormitory, and one for the girls'.

As buddies, Nick and Elliot stood together, waiting their turn to put their names on the register.

"Get a load of Coleman," whispered Nick. "He's walking around like a zombie."

"He's always been a heavy sleeper," grinned Elliot. "When he wakes up, it takes him half an hour to figure out what planet he's on."

The desk clerk was a young man with shoulder-length hair. He studied the guest book with a frown. "All right," he announced, "Who's the wise guy?"

"I beg your pardon?" asked Mrs. Montrose.

"One of your boys signed his name as Dan Marino."

Instantly, Mr. Sargent glared in the direction of Nick and Elliot. Anything concerning football usually came from the Monday Night Football Club.

"It wasn't us," they chorused.

The teacher's accusing gaze then singled out the student he thought was Coleman Galloway.

The confused Dolphin glared back, unafraid. "Well, what am I supposed to sign?"

"How about 'Coleman Galloway'?" seethed the teacher.

"Who's Coleman Galloway?" Marino demanded.

It got a big laugh from the Middletown students.

Mr. Sargent didn't think it was funny. "Follow me,

Coleman. We're going to have a discussion about proper behavior on a field trip!" He led Marino into the lobby.

Nick and Elliot flashed the Monday Night Football Club's "Sarge" salute. But their friend Coleman didn't seem to notice.

Nick's brow furrowed. "Signing his name Dan Marino? Mouthing off to Sarge? It sure doesn't sound like the Coleman *I* know."

"I have a theory about that," said Elliot. "Caitlin called him a chicken. So now he's showing her how fearless he is."

Nick nodded. "If he keeps this up, he'll be the most fearless guy ever to get kicked out of the fifth grade."

I Want to Report a Missing Person

California time was three hours earlier than the East Coast, so the kickoff was scheduled for three o'clock. At nine A.M. the team gathered in their hotel banquet room for breakfast.

Coleman stared at the huge mountain of scrambled eggs sitting at one end of his table.

"Wow," he said to big Zach Thomas, the Dolphins linebacker. "Do you really think we can eat all that?"

"We? What do you mean we? This is mine."

Coleman's mouth dropped open and stayed open. A parade of waiters marched in. They brought identical portions for each player. His server placed before him a plate of eggs that should have had its own zip code.

"Here you go, sir. Extra Tabasco sauce, just as you ordered it."

Coleman almost swallowed his tongue. "But my mother says I have a delicate stomach! I'm not allowed to eat anything too spicy!"

It got loud rumbling belly laughs from the Miami Dolphins.

Oh no! I'm making the great Dan Marino look like a clown!

So, in spite of his mother's warnings, Coleman shut his eyes and began to eat. When he opened them again, he found himself looking at a half-empty plate. *Maybe I can't handle spicy food*, he reflected, *but Dan Marino's stomach is made of fireproof asbestos!*

An hour later, Dan Marino's famous face, lathered with shaving cream, stared back from the mirror in the Dolphins locker room. Coleman stood with his razor in his hand—*Dan Marino's hand*—working up his courage for the first stroke.

Come on, he told himself. *If you're too much of a wimp to shave, how are you ever going to play in the Super Bowl?*

Here goes nothing—

Soon he was patting his bleeding chin with fistfuls of toilet paper.

"Dan, are you okay?" called Karim Abdul-Jabbar, the Dolphins star running back. "You look like you shaved with your eyes closed."

Coleman blushed. "I got a little carried away with my razor."

"Razor?" the star rusher repeated. "Nobody shaves for the Super Bowl!"

"But what if I get interviewed on TV?" asked Coleman.

Abdul-Jabbar laughed all the way down the tunnel. "Man, ever since *Ace Ventura, Pet Detective* you've gone Hollywood on us!"

With scraps of toilet paper on his many cuts, Coleman jogged out onto the field for the Dolphins' light workout.

Light! he shuddered. *If that's what they call light . . .*

It scared the heck out of him. At one point, Zach Thomas hit a tackling dummy so hard that the thing *exploded*! There was fluff and foam rubber everywhere. Maybe the real Dan Marino wasn't allergic to fuzz, but Coleman sure was. He started coughing, sneezing, and snorting so severely that he had to see the Dolphins' doctor.

So while his teammates got loose and limber, Coleman sat in the locker room, wheezing and drinking Gatorade with a thin layer of fluff on the surface.

"Hey, what happened to your chin?" the doctor asked in concern.

"My cat scratched me," mumbled Coleman, embarrassed. He hoped that Marino wasn't famous around the league as a cat hater. He didn't want to get his hero in trouble for lying.

A second, wilder thought struck him. *The real Dan Marino has problems of his own right now. He has to be partners with Matthew Leopold!*

In the Museum of Natural History in New York City, Dan Marino ducked behind the tyrannosaurus skeleton. He slipped away from the student tour and sidled over to the pay phone by the elevator.

He lifted the receiver and dialed his agent's cell phone number.

"Yeah?"

Marino could have wept at the sound of the familiar voice. It was proof that the whole world hadn't gone crazy.

"Kevin! I'm glad I caught you! It's Dan."

"Dan who?" the agent asked.

"Dan *Marino*!" the quarterback exclaimed.

"Yeah, right," the man snorted. "In twenty years, maybe. Listen kid, I don't know what you think you're doing, but this is my private line. Only my top clients call me here. My wife doesn't even have the number."

"But it's me!" Marino insisted. "This isn't my real voice. There's been an accident! Or a—I don't even know what you'd call it—a really weird thing!"

"I don't want to hear it," his agent cut him off. "Kid, this is the biggest day of my life. I'm in San Diego. In three hours my number one client is starring in the Super Bowl. If you phone me again, I'm calling the cops. Got it?"

He hung up.

Sweating—what kind of shirt was this? sandpaper?—he weighed his options. He couldn't call his friends or business associates. They'd just hear an eleven-year-old talking nonsense. There was only one thing left to do. He pressed the buttons *9-1-1*.

"Emergency operator."

"Yeah, hi. This is—uh, never mind who this is. I want to report a missing person."

"All right, son. Take it easy," soothed the woman. "Who's missing?"

"I am."

"What do you mean by missing? Are you lost? Have you been kidnapped?"

"Not exactly," Marino replied. "But—I'm not where I'm supposed to be."

"Oh." The operator sounded confused. "Well, how old are you, son?"

The quarterback frowned. "Thirty-six."

Click.

Okay, okay. No need to panic. There had to be a way to explain this. He picked up the phone for one last try.

"Emergency operator."

"Listen, I know I sound like a kid, but I'm a grown man. I'm a professional football player who's been changed into a fifth-grade boy. I don't know how it happened, but—"

Suddenly, the receiver was snatched from his hand and hung back on its cradle. He swung around and looked up into the concerned face of Mrs. Montrose.

"Coleman, what's gotten into you?" she demanded. "You've always been such a well-behaved boy. Is there something wrong?"

Hah! He couldn't describe his problem to his own agent and two 9-1-1 operators. How could he explain it to a fifth-grade teacher—even a nice one like this lady? He couldn't even explain it to himself!

"No, I'm fine," he said sadly.

He trailed after her, mumbling under his breath, "Oh, sure. Really fine. I'm eighteen inches too short, and I've never seen myself before in my life! I'm missing the Super Bowl—and, on top of it all, I've got the worst buddy in the whole fifth grade!"

"Where's my partner?" demanded Matthew Leopold.

"Where's Coleman?"

"Mrs. Montrose went to get him," replied Mr. Sargent patiently. "They'll be here in a minute. Then we can start the film."

Matthew's chalk-squeaking-on-a-blackboard voice seemed to echo through the minitheater. "He stinks at the buddy system! He should get lots of detentions."

Caitlin leaned over to Nick and Elliot. "What's with your friend Coleman? He's been in trouble all day."

"Oh, Coleman's in trouble all the time," Nick said cheerfully. "You think he's a chicken, but that's just an act. This is the real Coleman."

"He sure is different," she agreed. "All of a sudden, it's like he's a lot older than we are."

Mrs. Montrose came in and led Marino over to Matthew. The students sat down cross-legged on the floor as the lights dimmed in the theater.

As Marino settled himself and leaned forward, his sweater rode up in the back, revealing the brown wool of the Eskimos jersey underneath.

A couple of rows behind him, Elliot elbowed Nick in the ribs. "Did you see that?" he rasped.

Nick nodded. "I guess he had to wear it to sneak it out of the house this morning. Can you imagine the itch, having it right on your skin like that?"

Elliot was trembling with excitement. "Think, Nick! He fell asleep on the bus! He fell asleep *in the shirt*!"

Nick gasped. "You think he switched with somebody?"

Elliot nodded vigorously. "That's why he's acting so weird. He's not him!"

"How can we find out which player he switched with?" Nick breathed.

"That's easy," said Elliot. "I think he told us. Man, he tried to tell *everybody* when he signed in at the Y!"

"You mean to tell me that he signed Dan Marino because he *is* Dan Marino?"

Elliot nodded solemnly.

The movie began with loud music and spectacular special effects. But Nick and Elliot wouldn't have noticed if the dinosaurs had been real, in the theater, eating people. Two rows ahead of them sat the phenomenal all-pro Dolphins star—hero of big games, starting quarterback for the Super Bowl.

6

The Super-Duper Jumbo Mega-Fantastic Bowl

Middletown Elementary School ordered thirty pizzas with a wide variety of toppings. Nick and Elliot called it the Super Meal. They grabbed blindly at the buffet and sprinted ahead of the line to snag the two chairs directly in front of the TV.

"Fifteen minutes to kickoff!" whispered Elliot. "I can't believe Coleman's actually there!"

"I can't believe Dan Marino's actually *here!*" added Nick. "I mean, ten feet away, dumping hot chili peppers on his pizza!"

"What?" Elliot was shocked. "Maybe Marino likes hot food, but he doesn't know he's using Coleman's stomach!" He half rose out of his chair. "*Milk* is too spicy for Coleman. We'd better warn the guy."

Nick grabbed him by the sleeve. "Sit down and keep quiet!" he said under his breath. "We're not going to tell Dan Marino anything!"

Elliot looked surprised. "Why not?"

"Because we'd have to tell him why he's here and what's going on. And when all this is over, he'll report us to the NFL and they'll send the cops to take away our Eskimos jersey."

"There's no law against having a magic shirt, you know," Elliot pointed out.

"Only because no one's ever had one before," Nick insisted. "But when word gets around, it'll be illegal so fast it'll make your head spin!"

Elliot glared accusingly at Nick. "You are dooming the great Dan Marino to a gut-blaster stomachache!"

"It's not my fault," Nick reasoned. "Blame it on Coleman. Leave it to our dumb friend to take something so simple and mess it up! I mean, what could be easier? The game starts, you put on the shirt, you fall asleep. But no. He has to strand poor Dan Marino for a whole day."

"Now that you mention it," Elliot said solemnly, "what do you suppose Coleman's been up to in San Diego all this time?"

Nick groaned. "Let's hope he's got the brains to keep his big mouth shut. Because if they find out he's an impostor, they're going to hang him from the highest arc light in Qualcomm Stadium!"

* * *

Super was far too simple a word to describe the majesty of the Super Bowl.

They should call it the Super-Duper Jumbo Mega-Fantastic Bowl! thought Coleman as he waited with his teammates to be introduced.

It wasn't just the seventy thousand screaming fans or the battalions of reporters and photographers. It wasn't even the blaring music, or the fireworks, or the heart-stopping flyover by air force jets. It was the feeling that the entire world had ground to a halt. For the next few hours, the eyes of all humanity would be trained on this place—a hundred yards of manicured grass, for now the center of the universe.

". . . and at quarterback for the Dolphins, from the University of Pittsburgh, the man who has passed for more yards than anyone in NFL history, number thirteen—*Dan Marino!*"

What a feeling! Coleman ran through the honor guard of Dolphins, slapping hands, knees pumping high. He waved his helmet to the cheering crowd.

His real life—where he was too chicken to suit Caitlin Mooney, and where a creep like Matthew Leopold called him Coleslaw—seemed a trillion miles away. *He* was the person who stood there for the coin toss *right beside the president of the United States*! And when the toss came up heads just as he'd called it, he let out a joyous "Ya-*hoo!*" leaping high and punching the air. He felt a little foolish carrying on in front of an important guy like the president.

"I never win at anything," he confessed shyly. "Not since times-tables bingo in fourth grade."

The president said he understood how that felt. Then they shook hands, and the president said, "Good luck. I'm a fan."

Well, a fan of Dan Marino, anyway, Coleman thought. *But for a while today, that's me.*

"This has been the greatest day of my life!" he cried on the sidelines.

Coach Jimmy Johnson stared at him. "This day hasn't started yet. We're here to play a football game, remember?"

As if on cue, the ground shook beneath their feet. It wasn't an earthquake; the Super Bowl was on!

Coleman watched the kickoff return in awe. How could people so big move so fast? And the hits—bodies were flying in all directions! It was like planets colliding! *What kind of lunatic would go out there on purpose?*

Coach Johnson slapped him on the back. "Okay, Dan. You're up."

Fear. Doom. Terror. Panic. Horror.

Coleman's hands were shaking as he reached for the ball from between the center's stout legs. *I'm so scared!* he thought desperately. *Please don't let me faint in front of all these people!*

He swallowed hard and remembered his own words: "Quarterbacks have a wall of three-hundred-pound linemen protecting them."

"Hut!"

The snap slapped into his hands so hard that he almost dropped it. He took two steps back into the pocket and looked up. An appalling sight met his eyes. Yes, the three-hundred-pound protectors were there.

But he hadn't really thought about the big, tough, blitzing defenders on the other side of them.

He was never quite sure which linebacker hit him first. The monster from the left went low, driving his legs out from under him. The giant from the right rammed his shoulder into Coleman's face guard. The double tackle knocked him silly, and the ball flew out of his hands. One of the Green Bay defenders picked it up and ran into the end zone for a touchdown. Coleman was too dazed to tell if it was the monster or the giant who scored.

He reached up and pulled a huge clump of turf off his face guard. *One lousy play*, he thought miserably, *and I'm already half-dead and losing seven–zip.*

Blowout

In the YMCA dormitory, Mr. Sargent sat down on the bunk opposite the student he thought was Coleman Galloway.

"Rough day, huh?" he smiled sympathetically.

"You'll never know *how* rough," Marino replied. Now, on top of everything else, his stomach was killing him. He'd never suffered from heartburn in his life! Then again, he'd never been changed into somebody else, either.

"Look, Coleman," said the teacher. "I'm sorry I've been so hard on you today. I realize it must have been disappointing to be separated from your two friends because of the buddy system. But come on! How can a big fan like you miss the Super Bowl? You don't have to stick with Matthew. Nobody's going to stop you from sitting with Nick and Elliot."

Marino looked up. "What have they said on TV

about the disappearance of Dan Marino?"

Mr. Sargent chuckled. "I wouldn't say he's disappeared exactly. But I'll bet he wishes the ground would open up and swallow him. He's having a terrible first half."

The quarterback's eyes bulged. "You mean he's *there*?"

The teacher looked surprised. "Of course."

His aching stomach forgotten, Marino was up and out of the dormitory. He rounded the corner into the lounge and stopped dead. His jaw dropped. There, on the TV, was Dan Marino. At least, it *looked* like him.

But he was *here*! It was impossible! And yet, the evidence was right there on the twenty yard line of the Super Bowl!

"If *he's* me," he muttered out loud, "then who am *I*?"

He was so shaken up that he actually considered the possibility that he *wasn't* Dan Marino. Maybe he really *was* this Coleman What's-his-face from Whatevertown.

And his childhood in Pittsburgh, his career in football, his whole life—what was that? A dream? A hallucination?

"Hut, hut!"

Marino watched himself run in aimless terrified circles on the TV. And suddenly, it all became clear in his mind, like driving out of a thick fog on the highway.

No way was that chicken Dan Marino! He was an impostor! And the real Marino had to get to California to expose this fraud!

He ran out of the lounge, narrowly avoiding a collision with Mr. Sargent in the doorway.

"What about the game?" asked the teacher.

"Bathroom break," he called over his shoulder.

In front of the TV, Elliot nudged Nick. "Bathroom break," he repeated in a low voice. "I think all those chili peppers might be starting to do a number on Dan Marino."

"He doesn't need peppers to make him sick," Nick whispered back. "All he has to do is watch Coleman in the Super Bowl."

"We should have seen it coming," Elliot agreed sadly. "Coleman was too scared to throw with Lady Saliva coming at him. How could we expect him to stand up to the whole Packers defense?"

"How could we know?" Nick muttered unhappily. "I mean, you played like Barry Sanders; I played like John Elway. But Coleman's playing like *Coleman*!"

"He's got Marino's ability," Elliot mused. "But I guess he doesn't have the guts to use it."

Green Bay kicked a field goal to open up a 17–0

lead. Coleman had yet to complete a pass. The Super Bowl was turning into a blowout.

"I almost wish I'd never laid eyes on my grandpa's football shirt!" Nick lamented. Nicholas Farrel Lighter spent the entire year in breathless anticipation of this great day. At the closing gun of last year's big game, his brain had become fixed on *this* year's big game. And now, thanks to Coleman, the Monday Night Football Club was *ruining* the Super Bowl!

The clatter of cleats on cement was the only sound in the Dolphins locker room at halftime. Absent were the high fives and excited chatter of a football team in high gear. Instead, the players slumped against lockers and buried their heads in towels.

The Packers had completely dominated the first half. Led by two touchdown passes from quarterback Brett Favre, Green Bay was trouncing the Dolphins 27–0—the biggest halftime lead in Super Bowl history.

"What has happened to Dan Marino?" the play-by-play announcer asked on the small TV atop the row of lockers. "How could the greatest passer of all time have no completions *and only two attempts* in thirty minutes of play? What's even worse is it almost seems like he's *afraid* to throw the ball—"

A meaty hand switched off the set. Coleman looked up. Coach Johnson stood over him.

Coleman braced himself for a Super Bowl–size chewing out. Instead, the big man looked shocked. "Is something wrong, Dan? Are you hurt? Sick? Do you have a fever?"

Coleman wanted to cry. "I'm sorry, Coach—"

"Dan, we all have bad games, even on Super Bowl Sunday," Johnson went on. "But this is nuts! If I wasn't looking at you with my own two eyes, I'd swear you were somebody else. Not the tough guy from Pittsburgh with no fear and an arm like a cannon. I'd be a fool not to bench you right now! Think about it! Dan Marino yanked out of the Super Bowl."

He paused to let his words sink in. Assistant coaches and players looked on in awe.

"I've seen you succeed and I've seen you fail, but I never thought I'd see you too scared to try! Why"— Johnson shook his head in disbelief—"Dan, you're playing like a *chicken!*"

Face flaming red, Coleman drew himself up to Marino's full height. "I don't mind if you call *me* a chicken!" he told his coach. "But I refuse to let you say anything that rotten about Dan Marino!"

"You're also nuts," the coach added.

Coleman wheeled on his cleats and stormed out of the locker room. Half a dozen players leaped to their feet to stop him.

"Let him go," ordered Johnson.

"Do you think the pressure might have gotten to him?" asked Karim Abdul-Jabbar.

"We're in the Super Bowl thanks to that guy," said the coach of the Miami Dolphins. "We'll stick with him the rest of the way."

The halftime show was in full swing. The cement tunnel outside the locker room was packed full of high school band members and dancing girls in huge fluffy costumes.

"Hey, it's Dan Marino!"

Bobbing pink feathers brushed in his face, and trombones and bass drums whacked him in the shoulder pads. He plowed through the crush of people and instruments and stood at the field entrance.

The spectacular dance number glittered brighter than all the dazzle of Broadway and Hollywood combined. How many times had the Monday Night Football Club wallowed in every second of the Super Bowl halftime extravaganza, savoring it the way you'd lick the wrapper of a partly melted candy bar? Now Coleman was *here*—and he hardly noticed the strobe lights and fireworks and lasers. The only lights that mattered to Coleman were on the Qualcomm scoreboard—the ones that spelled out *27–0* for the Packers.

27–0! And the game was only half over! Dan Marino practically owned the record book. But would anybody think of that?

No! Coleman was in agony. *All they'll remember is that he played like a chicken in the Super Bowl!*

Dan Marino! Coleman's favorite player! His all-time hero!

I won't let it happen! Coleman decided. *Maybe I can't score twenty-seven points, but I can win back respect for Dan Marino!*

But how? He already had Marino's talent—and he stunk out the world!

The answer came from Coach Johnson's words: "the tough guy from Pittsburgh." And from Elliot: "quarterbacks have to be the toughest guys in the NFL."

It wasn't enough to have Marino's ability; he needed Marino's *toughness,* too—toughness to get off a throw even when he knew he was going to take a crushing hit.

Are you crazy? You'll get killed!

This time, it was Caitlin Mooney's voice that echoed

in his brain. "Everybody knows you're the biggest chicken in town."

Coleman gritted Marino's teeth. *Not anymore, Caitlin.*

No one—not even Coleman Galloway—was allowed to make a loser out of the great Dan Marino!

The Famous Marino Touch

To the west of the stadium, the sun was setting over the Pacific Ocean.

And in a few seconds, it might very well be setting on my broken neck, Coleman thought as he crouched behind the center. *I'm going to get creamed!*

"But I don't care," he said aloud, "because I'm doing it for Dan Marino!"

"What?" the center called nervously over his shoulder. "Are you calling an audible?"

"No!" he barked. "I'm changing my life! Hut, hut!"

He took the snap and dropped back three quick steps. The pounding of his heart shook Marino's whole body.

Forget the linebackers, Coleman ordered himself. *Ignore the safeties. Throw!*

He reared back his arm and unloaded with all his might. The ball took off like a cruise missile. It was still rising as it sailed far above the heads of the sprinting receivers. It cleared the end zone, passed dead center between the goalposts, and landed in the upper deck of Qualcom Stadium.

Coleman was astounded. "Wow!" he breathed. "Did you see that?"

"Great," Karim Abdul-Jabbar said sarcastically. "Too bad that guy sitting in row thirty-five isn't one of our receivers."

I always knew Marino had a great arm, he marveled. *But that's not the same as actually throwing with it. It's like having a rocket launcher growing out of your shoulder!*

So he had Marino's arm. And for the first time, he felt something else that belonged to the all-pro quarterback.

Marino's confidence. *I can do this*, he told himself.

Fred Barnett jogged into the huddle with the next play-call from Coach Johnson. Coleman couldn't hide his disappointment. It was a run.

But I want to try out this passing arm! he felt like screaming.

Then, at the line of scrimmage, it hit him. *I'm the quarterback. I can change the play.*

Instantly, the Dolphin playbook laid itself out in Dan Marino's orderly mind. He picked the gutsiest pass pattern of them all.

"Blue eighty-seven!" he bellowed so loud that his

lungs hurt. His voice had to reach the receivers over the roar of the crowd. "Blue eighty-seven!"

From his position wide right, O. J. McDuffie stared at him. "Are you crazy?" he cried. "You couldn't hit the side of a barn today!"

But Coleman would not be denied. "Blue eighty-seven!" he yelled again. "Hut, hut, hut!"

He took the snap, dropped back, and scanned the field. McDuffie was streaking down the sidelines.

Coleman's heart leaped. *This is it!*

He threw—not as hard as before, but with *touch*.

The famous Marino touch.

Wham! Green Bay's Reggie White ran into Coleman like a speeding bus. Coleman went down hard, but he barely noticed the pain. He jumped back up just in time to watch his perfect pass drop into McDuffie's outstretched hands in the end zone.

The referee raised his arms. "Touchdown!"

The stadium exploded with deafening cheers. The loyal Miami fans—quiet for the first half—came alive.

On the sidelines, Coach Johnson gave Coleman a lopsided smile. "I guess I should chew you out for changing the play."

Zach Thomas enfolded him in a mammoth bear hug. "Welcome back, Dan."

* * *

In the bathroom of the Manhattan YMCA, Elliot Rifkin splashed water on his face. Super Bowl Sunday, the most awesome day of the year, was a Super Disaster. He and Nick never should have forced Coleman to try out the Eskimos shirt. Either one of them could have taken his place today. Heck, they would have *fought* for the chance to play in the Super Bowl!

He inspected his reflection in the mirror. A familiar shade of brown caught his eye. He wheeled. There, wadded up in the corner of the bathroom, was the Eskimos sweater.

He chuckled. "Even the toughest quarterback in football can't stand the itch of—" His breath caught in his throat. Where was Dan Marino?

He picked up the jersey and ran into the boys' dormitory. It was empty. There was a roar in the TV lounge. Head spinning, he burst through the door. The fifth graders were on their feet, clapping and cheering.

"What's going on?" he asked.

"Marino just threw an eighty-yard touchdown pass!" called Mr. Sargent.

"Marino?" Elliot repeated. "You mean"—he turned to Nick and hissed—"Coleman?"

"Yeah!" Nick marveled. "And he took a bone-crusher

hit and just popped right back up! He's getting the hang of it!"

"It's too bad your friend Coleman wasn't here to see it," put in Mrs. Montrose.

"Where *is* Coleman?" added Mr. Sargent.

Lies didn't come easily to straight, logical Elliot. But this was an emergency. "He—he's taking a nap."

"What a lousy buddy!" piped up Matthew. "He can't even stay awake on Super Bowl Sunday!"

"Hey!" snapped Elliot. "The guy's got a stomach-ache! Too many peppers on his pizza." Well, at least that was probably true.

Nick sidled over. "Really?" he whispered. "Dan Marino is sleeping through the Super Bowl?"

"I wish." With his eyes, Elliot drew his friend's attention down to the old brown sweater clenched in his sweating hands.

Nick sucked in a sharp gasp. "You think he took off?"

Elliot nodded. "He must have ducked into the bath-room, ditched the shirt, and bolted."

"But where could he go?" Nick asked in a shaky voice. "I mean, *we* know he's Dan Marino. But every-body else will see an eleven-year-old kid wandering around New York City! We've got to find him!"

"That's the *worst* thing we could do," insisted Elliot.

"Then we'd have three lost kids instead of just one. We don't know New York!"

"Neither does poor Dan Marino," Nick pointed out.

"Poor Dan Marino?" echoed Elliot. "When all this is over, he returns to his own body in San Diego. It's *Coleman* who's going to land right smack dab in the middle of whatever mess Dan gets into. He could wind up lost on the subway. He could come back to himself in the middle of being mugged. And if Marino tries to tell anybody who he really is, Coleman could go straight from the Super Bowl to the nuthouse!"

"Oh no!" Nick moaned. "What are we going to do?"

"First we have to sneak into the dormitory and jam some pillows into Coleman's bunk," whispered Elliot. "If Sarge looks in there, he'd better not see an empty bed."

"Then what?"

Elliot shrugged. "We wait."

Nick was appalled. "We do *nothing*?"

"He's a fifth grader with a little souvenir money and a story straight out of *Ripley's Believe It or Not*. If we're lucky, he'll get tired of people ignoring him, and he'll come back here."

"And if we're *un*lucky?" Nick quavered.

Elliot laughed without humor. "The end of the world. But at least it will come on Super Bowl Sunday."

9

A Super Fumble

The game unfolded like a three-act drama. Act one had been all Packers. That set the stage for act two, where the Dolphins came fighting back. On a play-action rollout, Coleman hit Karim Abdul-Jabbar with a twenty-yard pass. The slippery runner danced into the end zone, narrowing the gap to 27–14. But the spectacular touchdown marked the beginning of act three—a clinic on perfect defense by Green Bay.

Tight coverage gave Coleman nowhere to throw. All-out blitzes led to sacks and holding penalties. Drive after drive ended in punt after punt.

Coleman felt terrible. If he hadn't blown the entire first half, Miami might very well be tied or maybe even in the lead. He watched in despair as the Packers ground their way down the field, eating up the clock. Six minutes, five, then four. Antonio Freeman caught a pass to bring Green Bay within field goal range.

And then Zach Thomas showed why he was one of

the most feared young players in the league. The quick linebacker caught Freeman from behind, wrapping him up with an arm like a tree trunk. Thomas's free hand grabbed for the ball—snatching, digging, pounding—

"*Fumble!!*" Coleman shrieked. Brown leather disappeared beneath a pile of flying bodies.

Chaos! Struggle! And then . . . celebrating Dolphins.

Hope.

"It's the ultimate test of a quarterback," the play-by-play announcer raved over the TV in the YMCA. "Marino versus the defensive backs, Marino versus the blitz—"

"It's also Marino versus the clock," put in the color commentator. "He needs two touchdowns in less than three minutes. So he's even fighting time itself."

Elliot shook his head in disbelief. "If they only knew they were talking about the chicken of Middletown Elementary School."

"Not anymore," Nick said firmly. "Man, the next time some guy calls our friend a wimp, remind me to punch him in the face!" He pointed to the screen. "Look at how Coleman's standing up to the pressure— throwing sideline passes so his receivers can get out of bounds. I can't believe that's the same kid who was afraid of Lady Saliva!"

"Another first down!" cried the announcer. "But the clock is ticking! Will time run out on the Dolphins? One thing is for certain: none of the loyal Miami fans has given up on Dan Marino!"

"That's not true!" piped up Matthew. "Coleslaw gave up way back in the first quarter. He was too much of a wimp to watch his precious Dolphins lose!"

Nick and Elliot leaped up and wheeled to face Matthew.

"You take that back!" roared Nick.

"Why should I?" sneered Matthew. "It's the truth!"

"Hey! Hey!" Mr. Sargent stepped forward. "No fighting! We're trying to watch a football game, right?"

Nick was about to snap back at Matthew when he heard a roar from the TV.

"Touchdown!"

Forty-nine fifth graders crowded around the set for the replay. Even the teachers were hooked. It was incredible—Miami had closed the gap to six points.

"They're dead meat!" snorted Matthews. "They have to kick off to the Packers, right? There are only forty seconds left. Green Bay can just run out the clock!"

"That shows how much *you* know!" Nick shot back. "What about an onside kick?"

"What's that?" asked Caitlin.

"One of the most amazing plays in football,"

explained Elliot, vibrating with excitement. "Instead of a long kickoff, you boot the ball ten yards and send your fastest guys to recover it!"

"I can't believe we're going to see it in a Super Bowl!" Nick added breathlessly.

Sure enough, the Dolphins' "hands" team lined up in tight formation beside the kicker. To make this squad, a player needed both speed and strength—and a grip like the jaws of a crocodile.

Nick and Elliot held their breath. Three thousand miles away, in Dan Marino's uniform, they knew their friend Coleman was doing the same.

The squib kick rolled about twelve yards. It took a strange high bounce. From opposite directions, both teams sprinted underneath the spinning ball. They met with a crunch, pushing and shoving for position. The kick came down. It bounced off a helmet and passed through a tangle of wrestling arms.

"It's anybody's ball!" cried Elliot.

The whistle blew, and the officials began unraveling the forest of girder-thick arms. Both teams were signaling possession for their side. But when the referee finally dug out the football . . .

"First down, Miami!" bawled the announcer.

Exactly thirty-three seconds remained on the clock.

I'm Going to Disney World

Qualcomm Stadium seemed ready to wrench free of its foundation and blast off for Jupiter. All seventy thousand seats were empty—*everyone* was standing. The pounding and stomping caused ripples in the Gatorade bucket. It was the kind of noise that seeped in through the skin and rattled your bones—the roar of a crowd that could almost taste the greatest Super Bowl comeback of all time.

Coleman looked at the circle of faces around him in the huddle: Karim-Abdul-Jabbar, O. J. McDuffie, Fred Barnett—

These great stars are turning to me for inspiration! Me! The chicken of Middletown Elementary School. What can I say to them? What would Dan Marino say?

Coleman thought about his hero's boyish but intense look. Marino always resembled a kid who was happy but *focused*—like the Monday Night Football Club psyching up for a tough trick play.

Coleman forced that expression onto Marino's face. "This is what we've practiced for," he said with a confidence he was far from feeling. "Let's do it."

The drive started with a bullet pass to McDuffie. Then Coleman lofted a floater to Abdul-Jabbar, streaking down the sidelines.

"Go!" screamed Coleman as the ball dropped right into the young star's hands.

Then it was a blur—a diving cornerback, the *crack* of two helmets colliding, the loose football bouncing on the turf.

Seventy thousand spectators gulped in air like a titanic vacuum cleaner. Abdul-Jabbar pounced on his own fumble to save the day.

Coleman dropped to his knees, weak with relief. His bliss lasted three seconds.

"The clock, Dan!" bellowed Coach Johnson from the sidelines. *"The clock's still running!"*

What? Oh no! There were only ten seconds left!

"Line up!" Coleman shrieked to his teammates, sprinting for the ball.

The scoreboard ticked down. *Six . . . five . . . four . . .*

Dolphins scrambled from all over the field. The

Green Bay defenders took their sweet time getting back. It was their plan to run out the clock before Miami could try another play.

...three ... two ... one ...

One Packer, while strolling to his position, bumped into Coleman. Another "accidentally" stepped on the ball, knocking it out of the center's hands. The center rushed to set it up again.

"Hut!" cried Coleman.

But right at the snap, the whistle blew. Coleman deflated like a balloon. The Super Bowl was over.

"No-o-o-o-o!" he wailed.

Suddenly, the P.A. system sprang to life. "Flag on the play."

The referee held out his arms. "Unsportsmanlike conduct. Kicking the ball prior to the snap—"

Coleman's heart soared. The game wasn't over after all! The Packers' move had backfired!

A football game can't end on a defensive penalty! Coleman remembered. "We get another chance!" he yowled, jumping high in the air.

The referee marched the ball ahead fifteen yards. One final second was put on the clock. *That single tick,* thought Coleman, *could change the course of Super Bowl history!*

He crouched under his center. Now the stadium was strangely silent. His "Hu-u-u-ut!" felt like a ten-syllable word. He dropped back and scanned the field with Marino's eagle eyes. And he saw . . .

Nothing!

Where are my receivers? Coleman wanted to howl.

With the game hanging in the balance, Green Bay's defense was as solid as Hoover Dam.

Receivers—covered. Tight ends—covered. Running backs—covered. Why, the only player without a Packer breathing down his neck was—

Coleman's breath caught in his throat—*me!*

He tucked away the ball and sprinted for the goal line. The legendary Dan Marino didn't run very often. But he always did whatever it took to win. And tonight so would Coleman Galloway.

Breathing hot fire, he aimed Marino's long legs at the orange pylon at the corner of the end zone. Not one, not two, but three big Packer defenders zeroed in on him.

Coleman's heart was pounding in his throat. *Three unblocked men on a quarterback!* Even in years of football watching, the Monday Night Football Club had never seen it. It was going to be a massacre!

I've got to run out of bounds! he panicked.

But the Dolphins would lose.

Better to lose the Super Bowl than your life!

Then something strange happened. Coleman blinked, and the three fierce Packers disappeared. For an instant, they were replaced by Lady Godiva, the loving Saint Bernard, bounding toward him in the Saliva Blitz Pocket Fire Pass.

And who's afraid of a little dog drool? thought Coleman.

With a cry of *"Dolphins!"* he hurled himself at the goal line.

Wham!

Eight hundred pounds of Packer knocked Coleman back like a bowling pin. A split second before hitting the turf, he thrust the football out in front of him. The nose of the ball *just* brushed the inside of the pylon. Then the three flying defenders came back to earth right on top of him.

"Touchdown!" cried the referee, raising both hands.

Am I dead? I think I'm probably dead.

Coleman found himself back on the bench, but he had no idea how he'd managed to get there. Thinking was pretty tough when your body felt as flat as a pancake. Breathing took all the effort he could manage—and he wasn't doing a very good job of that, either. He was seeing double. On the field, two Dolphin kicking teams were lining up in front of two sets of goalposts. The two scoreboards read 2727–2727. . . Was that reasonable?

Wait a minute. . . .

The importance of this kick came crashing down on Coleman like a meteorite. His vision cleared in a heartbeat. Never before had the Super Bowl come down to a single extra point.

All at once, the simple play was anything but automatic. The goalposts seemed about three feet wide. The ball was made of stone, and the Packers were all nine feet tall.

Holder John Kidd's "Hut!" sounded squeaky and uncertain—like it was coming from a lost five-year-old in a crowded mall. Defenders jumped. Blocking arms soared like totem poles. Joe Nedney's kick went up at a sharp angle, rising toward the left upright.

Oh no! lamented Coleman. Terrible images flashed through his mind. The extra point would be no good; the Super Bowl would go into overtime; the Packers would blow them away. . . .

The world stood still as the ball closed in on the goalpost. Then, at the last second, the kick bended in a tiny hook and slipped just inside the upright.

Final score: 28–27 Miami. Fireworks. Celebration. Chaos.

Or was it 2828–2727? What was going on here? He was seeing double again!

The field lurched and swung up to meet him.

A blast of cold liquid brought Coleman back to life.

He squirmed. "Cut it out, Nick! Leave me alone, Elliot!"

Another icy shower sent him into shivers.

Wait a minute. This smells funny. This isn't water!

His eyes popped open. The locker room was insanity. Players and coaches were embracing each other and screaming. Teammates were waving bottles, and champagne was spraying in all directions. It was the Super Bowl celebration—a joyous bubbly crossfire.

"Hey, watch it! I'm not old enough for champagne!"

He got a faceful of the stuff in reply.

A TV camera was pointed at him, so he bellowed, "*I'm going to Disney World!*"

What else do you say when you win the big one? Of course, it would be the *real* Dan Marino making that trip. Coleman would be headed—

That's when it hit him. The Super Bowl was over, and he was still *here*—and still Dan Marino! The magic of the Eskimos shirt wasn't supposed to last past the game!

How was he ever going to get back to himself?

Why Aren't You *You*?

The night manager of the Manhattan YMCA glared at Nick and Elliot. "Quiet, you two," he insisted. "Otherwise, I'm going to have to report you to your teachers."

"But didn't you see the Super Bowl?" rasped Nick, out of breath from dancing and cheering. "Didn't you see that amazing come-from-behind win?"

"We've got a small TV behind the desk," the man nodded. "It was a great game."

"*Great?!*" Elliot howled in disbelief. "'Great' is an insult to the most astounding, fantastic, out-of-control—"

"Shhhh!" The man held a finger to his lips. "No more yelling! And no more whistling, hooting, high fives, stomping, or banging on the walls. Sheesh! It's not the first time Dan Marino was a hero."

The man walked away, shaking his head. With effort, they calmed down. They would never be able to explain it to the manager: this may have been a normal day at the office for Marino, but it was a miracle times fifty for the chicken of Middletown Elementary School. And for his two best friends.

Nick checked his watch. "Coleman must be himself again by now. I hope he gets here before somebody notices he's gone."

No sooner were the words out of his mouth than Matthew's voice rang out in the dormitory. "Guess what, Coleslaw? You missed the Super Bowl!"

Uh-oh.

They peered into the darkened room. Matthew was standing over Coleman's bunk. "Come on, wake up!" He yanked off the covers and gawked at the pile of pillows underneath. "Mr. Sargent! Mrs. Montrose! Coleman's gone!"

The two teachers were nowhere to be found. Instead, the entire fifth grade came running into the dormitory.

"Oh, no!" cried Caitlin. "What happened to Coleman?"

"What do we do now?" whispered Nick.

Before Elliot could reply, the night manager approached them once more. "Hey, have you savages got a Nick or an Elliot in your class?"

"It's us," Elliot replied breathlessly.

"Telephone. Some guy named Coleman."

They broke speed records to the pay phone in the hall. Nick got there just in time to hear a deep voice exclaim, "Ow!"

"Oh—sorry, mister," Nick said into the receiver. "I thought you were my friend Coleman."

"It's me. I stubbed my toe on the phone booth door," Coleman explained. "It's not easy walking around in size twelve shoes when you're used to kid feet."

"Coleman?!" Nick put two and two together. "You're still Dan Marino? Why aren't you *you*?"

Elliot stuck his ear right up beside Nick's. He was just in time to hear the famous voice declare, "What kind of friends are you guys, anyway? You lied. You said I'd be me again when the game ended!"

Elliot snapped his fingers. "I know what went wrong! Marino took off the shirt before he left!"

"Left?" choked Coleman. "What do you mean, he left?"

Nick swallowed hard. "I don't want to scare you, buddy. But right now, your body is out there somewhere wandering around the city of New York."

"You don't want to scare me?" Coleman cried. *"You're scaring me!"*

"Take it easy—," Elliot began.

"There's nothing easy to take!" Coleman moaned.

"What am I supposed to tell my mother? That I ate my Wheaties and I look like Dan Marino from now on? How could it be worse?"

At that moment, Matthew ran around the corner into the hall. "You guys are in *big* trouble!" he grinned.

"Who's that? Matthew?" asked Coleman. "Tell him to get lost! Tell him I'm six foot four!"

"You said Coleslaw was asleep!" sneered Matthew. "You lied!"

Nick stuck out his chin. "How do you know?"

"Because he's at the *airport*," Matthew blabbed.

"Says who?" challenged Elliot.

"Mr. Sargent, that's who!"

"You're delirious!" Nick accused. "Sarge would never talk about anything like that in front of a blabbermouth like you."

"He would so," retorted Matthew. "Besides, he didn't know I was listening. I heard him through the office door when I went to squeal on Coleslaw. He was on the phone with the police."

"The police?" they chorused.

Their horror made Matthew's smile wider. "They caught your crazy friend sneaking aboard a plane to San Diego. And guess what? That nutcase tried to tell them he was Dan Marino!"

"No way!" scoffed Elliot.

Matthew pointed out the window. "Mr. Sargent and Mrs. Montrose are going to get him right now."

Nick and Elliot stared. In the street below, the two teachers were climbing into a yellow taxicab.

"Told you so!" And Matthew ran off into the dormitory, yelling, "Hey, Caitlin! Guess where Coleslaw is *right now*!"

"What's going on?" Coleman demanded. "Dan Marino took *my body* to the *airport*?"

"If we can beat the teachers out there, maybe we could touch him with the sweater," Nick said thoughtfully. "That might switch you back."

Elliot shook his head. "He was wearing it right on his skin all day and nothing happened."

"Well, how did it work when you guys unswitched?" asked Coleman.

"The game ended—," Nick began thoughtfully.

"We both took big hits—," mused Elliot.

"But I took the biggest hit of all," Coleman protested. "I got knocked silly by three gorillas, and I didn't unswitch."

"I've got it!" Elliot was triumphant. "Right when Nick got tackled on *Monday Night Football*, John Elway smacked his head on the attic ceiling."

"Wait a minute!" Nick exclaimed. "When you got nailed, my sister elbowed Barry Sanders in the face!"

Coleman was confused. "So what?"

"So you and Dan Marino both have to get whacked at the same time!" Elliot explained.

"But who's going to hit Dan Marino?" Coleman cried.

Elliot rolled his eyes. "*We* are, dummy! Look, it's ten o'clock—seven, California time. It'll take us maybe half an hour to get to the airport. At exactly seven thirty, you give yourself a wallop—and make it a good one! We'll handle Dan Marino."

"That's the stupidest idea I've ever heard in my life!" Coleman exploded. "It's—like, straight out of a bad movie!"

"It's our only hope," Nick decided. "If we lose track of Dan Marino, you'll *never* get your old life back!"

Nick hung up. Elliot was already running for their coats.

They snuck past the manager at the front desk and ran out into the New York night. From dozens of open windows, the happy sounds of Super Bowl parties mingled in the crisp, cold air.

"I've always wanted to do this," Elliot said with a wild grin. He stepped off the curb, raised his arm, and bellowed, "*Yo, taxi!*"

Instantly, a streak of yellow screeched to a halt in front of them. Nick and Elliot climbed in.

"We're going to Kennedy airport," Nick told the cabbie. "And would it be possible to go really, really fast?"

The driver laughed. "Are you kidding? This is a New York City cab." He stomped on the gas, and the car disappeared in a squeal of burning rubber.

The Vince Lombardi Trophy

Coleman paced back and forth in the employee parking lot of Qualcomm Stadium. He squinted at Marino's watch. 7:22. In his other hand he held a small dumbbell from the training room. He had just eight more minutes to work up the courage to whack himself over the head with it.

If I don't do it hard enough, I won't switch back, he thought nervously. *But if I really smash it down I could hurt Dan Marino!*

And if this didn't work, Coleman might be spending the rest of his life as Dan Marino with a fractured skull.

He heard the heavy metal door behind him. "I guess it's time to go," said someone. "We've interviewed all the Dolphins except Dan Marino."

Wait a minute! I know that voice!

Coleman wheeled. It was Frank Gifford from *Monday Night Football*! He was working at the Super

Bowl with a camera crew from NFL Films.

One of the technicians pointed at Coleman. "Hey, isn't that Marino over there?"

Quickly, Coleman dropped the dumbbell. He watched helplessly as it rolled under a fence. But before he could react, Gifford and his crew were upon him.

"Dan, we've been looking all over for you," the Hall of Famer told him. "Can you give us a few minutes?"

Coleman was in agony. How could any Monday Night Football Club member turn down an interview with the great Frank Gifford? But it was already 7:25. "Well, uh, I've kind of got something I have to do—"

"It'll only take a few minutes," Gifford assured him.

"But—"

The cameraman switched on the floodlights.

Horns honked. Motorists cursed. But nobody moved. The taxi sat on the packed expressway outside Kennedy airport.

"How can there be a traffic jam *now*?" wailed Nick. "It's the middle of the night!"

"Welcome to New York," the cabbie said cheerfully.

"It's 10:27," moaned Elliot. "If we're not there in three minutes, we could lose Coleman forever!"

The two fifth graders exchanged horrified glances.

Could this be end of the Monday Night Football Club? The Eskimos shirt was better than fantastic, but it wasn't worth Coleman's whole life!

Nick's gaze shifted from his friend to the other taxi stopped beside them on the highway. He froze. There, in the back, sat Mr. Sargent and Mrs. Montrose.

"Duck!" he cried.

He squeezed into the space behind the front seat, pulling Elliot down with him. Elliot covered their heads with the Eskimos shirt.

"Hey," the driver called nervously over his shoulder. "Are you kids in some kind of trouble?"

"Those are our teachers in the next cab!" came Nick's muffled voice from under the sweater. "If they see us, we're dead!"

The man sighed. "I'd better get a really good tip for this!" He spun the steering wheel, and the taxi pulled onto the soft shoulder. The car flew past the snarled traffic, zoomed through the exit, and lurched to a halt in front of the airport.

The door opened, and out burst Nick and Elliot at a dead run. They sprinted into the building and stopped, scanning the terminal desperately.

Elliot pointed. "There!"

It was Dan Marino, still in Coleman's body. He sat

dejectedly on a bench between two airport security officers.

"Tell me, Dan," Frank Gifford was saying, "how did you
feel at halftime knowing you trailed the Packers by
twenty-seven points?"

"Well, uh, not too good, uh, Mr. Gifford." Coleman
stared past the microphone down to the watch on his
wrist. 7:29.

"Did you doubt your ability to come back?" Gifford
persisted.

But Coleman was transfixed. He followed the second hand as it rounded the dial toward 7:30. *How am I
going to hit myself?*

He looked around with wild eyes. The dumbbell was
under the fence and out of reach. The microphone was
too small.

"I, uh—" Ten seconds . . . five . . .

He looked up to the California sky. *Oh, please!* he
begged. *Please send me something I can use to get home!*

The metal door opened, and out stepped Jimmy
Johnson. In his burly arms the coach cradled the most
coveted object in football—the Vince Lombardi Super
Bowl trophy.

"Dan?" prompted Gifford.

"I—I—I'm sorry!" Coleman broke away from the interview and made a bull run at his coach—and the beautiful, wonderful, *heavy* object in his hands.

Dan Marino looked up at the officer on his right. "Hey, do you guys happen to know who won the Super Bowl?"

The man glared at him. "We're not 'you guys,' son. We're airport security agents."

"I'll bet the Dolphins lost," Marino said glumly. "They were playing like garbage."

"The Dolphins *won*," the other man told him. "Dan Marino led an incredible comeback."

"I did?—I mean, he did?" The quarterback looked up. All at once, his eyes fell on Nick and Elliot, charging across the concourse.

Those two kids from the school trip! How did they get here? And why were they running at him with that itchy shirt?

He jumped to his feet. "What the—"

"Now!" cried Nick.

They dove like linebackers, holding the Eskimos sweater out in front of them. The brown jersey struck Marino in the face, bowling him over backward.

Wham! He hit the floor hard. Nick and Elliot came crashing down on top of him.

"I'm sorry, Dan," whispered Nick.

Elliot pointed. "Look!"

It was the tiny glowing football, dancing over the brown fabric. It traced out the number *13*.

"Hey!" The two security agents yanked Nick and Elliot to their feet. One man pulled the sweater from Coleman's still form.

"Kid, are you okay?"

"Coleman, is that you?" added Nick.

Coleman didn't move.

Then a third voice rang out in the terminal. *"Coleman Galloway, get up off the floor this instant!"*

With a shudder, Coleman popped up and tried to hide himself behind Nick and Elliot. Mr. Sargent stormed across the concourse like a blitzing linebacker. Mrs. Montrose had to scramble to keep pace.

"You've got a *lot* of explaining to do, young man!" the teacher roared.

Mrs. Montrose looked at him in concern. "Why are there scratches all over your face?"

Still dazed, Coleman reached up to his chin. He ran his fingers along several short, straight scabs.

From the razor! I've still got the nicks I made on Dan Marino's face!

"I cut myself shaving," he replied honestly.

Mr. Sargent's face flamed bright red. "I've had it up to here with your smart mouth, Coleman! You've broken every rule in the book, talked back, run away—and even gotten yourself arrested! Your parents are going to have a *lot* to say about this when we get back to Middletown!" He turned to the two agents. "Officers, I'm so sorry about this. Are we free to take him back to the Y?"

"Please," smiled the senior man. "And keep an eye on him, okay?"

Nick and Elliot sidled up to their friend.

"Welcome home, hero," grinned Nick.

"I wasn't sure you'd make it," Elliot whispered. "What did you use to clobber yourself?"

Coleman let out the breath he'd been holding since the very moment he had put on the Eskimos jersey that morning. "Guys," he said, "you wouldn't believe me if I told you!"

The MVP

The itchy sweater was in his suitcase this time, instead of against his skin. But that did nothing to make the bus ride home any more comfortable for Coleman. He sat, halfway off the bench, leaning out into the aisle. He was keeping as much distance as possible between himself and Matthew Leopold.

"Mr. Sargent! Mrs. Montrose! Coleman's avoiding me!"

"He'll get his punishment soon enough," Mr. Sargent promised.

"And then some," added Mrs. Montrose.

Nick and Elliot sat near the front, watching the *Sport Report* on Nick's handheld TV.

"Poor Coleman," sighed Elliot. "Did you hear that Sarge called his folks last night? I'll bet they're *steaming!*"

Nick shrugged. "He played in the *Super Bowl*! He'll

take the heavy heat, but it's got to be worth it. Hey, I want to wear the Eskimos shirt for the Super Bowl next season. I called it."

"Okay," agreed Elliot. "But I get week one of *Monday Night Football*."

They turned their attention to the small screen. "And that wraps up our sports news today," the reporter was saying. "But we wanted to leave you with one final film clip. We think this will be televised year after year to illustrate the kind of craziness the Super Bowl brings out in people. Here's Frank Gifford interviewing Dan Marino after yesterday's big win."

They watched, thrilled. Their friend hadn't mentioned being interviewed by a *Monday Night Football* commentator!

"Hey, look." Elliot pointed. "It's Coleman's panic face. It looks kind of weird attached to Dan Marino!"

They goggled. Right in the middle of the interview, the Super Bowl quarterback ran to Jimmy Johnson and wrenched the Lombardi trophy from his hands. With a resounding *clang*, he conked the big silver football down on his head.

Nick was thunderstruck. "Well, at least we know what he used to hit himself last night."

"I've heard of making the most of a Super Bowl

championship, but this is ridiculous!" added Elliot, wide-eyed.

Coleman dreaded getting home. To him, the four-hour ride was over in the blink of an eye.

In the school parking lot, Mr. Sargent thanked the students for their good behavior on the trip. "We're pleased that *most* of you conducted yourselves with maturity." He cast a toxic look at Coleman.

Coleman faced his fellow Monday Night Football Club members. "Well, I guess I'll see you guys tomorrow. You know, if my parents don't kill me tonight."

Elliot laughed. "Look on the bright side. Your chicken reputation is gone forever."

"No, it isn't," he muttered. "Nobody knows I won the Super Bowl except you guys."

"Yeah, but what about all that stuff Dan Marino did?" Nick reminded him. "Mouthing off, running away, sneaking onto a plane to California—the whole fifth grade thinks that was you! You're going to be a legend at this school! I'll bet if you asked Caitlin to be your buddy *now*, she'd jump at the chance!"

"Big deal," scoffed Coleman. "The trip's over."

"Yeah, but the science fair is coming up next month," Elliot reminded him. "She's going to need a lab partner."

"You're right!" Coleman stood a little taller. "You know what? I'll do it!"

He marched over to where Caitlin stood with a group of friends. "Caitlin—" It was amazing! He wasn't nervous at all. After playing in a Super Bowl, talking to this popular girl was *nothing*! "Caitlin, do you want to be my lab partner for the science fair?"

She studied her sneakers. "I'd love to, but—"

"But what?" he prompted.

"Well," she looked straight into his eyes, "I don't think it's a good idea for me to get involved with your kind of wild crowd. I mean, look at yourself, Coleman. You're practically a juvenile delinquent!" And she walked away with her friends.

Nick and Elliot each put an arm around Coleman's shoulders.

"Women," shrugged Nick. "You can't win."

"Are you kidding?" The ex-chicken of Middletown Elementary School felt a wide grin bending his lips. "I was the Super Bowl MVP! Man, with NFL football, you can't lose!"

The Official Monday Night Football Club Story of Dan Marino, the Ultimate Quarterback

The portion of the *NFL Record & Fact Book* that includes passing totals could be called the *Dan Marino Pages*. In fifteen seasons with the Miami Dolphins, Marino has set nearly all of the important career passing records. He has thrown and completed more passes, for more yards and touchdowns, than any other passer in NFL history. Known for his quick release, his coolness under pressure, and his powerful arm, Marino is one of the best quarterbacks of all time.

Dan Marino was born 15 September 1961 in Pittsburgh. When he was eight years old, Marino was a ball boy for the Central Catholic High School football team. When he got older, he became the team's quarterback. He was also a star baseball player and was drafted by the Kansas City Royals after high school. Marino stayed near his home for college, attending the University of Pittsburgh. In four years at Pittsburgh, Marino broke all the school's major passing records and was named All-American. The Dolphins drafted him with the twenty-seventh pick in the first round of the 1983 NFL draft. Five other quarterbacks were chosen before Marino that year, including John Elway and Jim Kelly.

As a rookie, Marino quickly showed he was one of the best. He became the first rookie to start the Pro Bowl and was named NFL rookie of the year. His second season, 1984, was even better. In fact, it was one of the best seasons ever for an NFL quarterback. Marino passed for an NFL-record 5,084 yards and threw forty-eight touchdown passes, another all-time best. He led the Dolphins to their first AFC title since 1973 and to Super Bowl XIX.

In nearly every season since, Marino has been near the top of the NFL passing leaders. He has led the NFL in completions, attempts, passing yardage, and touchdown passes several times. He has thrown twenty or more touchdown passes in each of twelve seasons, four more than second-place Johnny Unitas. He has had eleven 3,000-yard seasons, tied for the most ever with Elway. Marino's outstanding passing, leadership, and enthusiasm have made him one of the league's most popular players.

All the while, Marino has been making his march on NFL passing records. He reached one hundred touchdown passes in his forty-fourth NFL game, the fastest anyone has hit that mark. He also was the fastest ever to reach 40,000 yards passing and three hundred touchdown passes. In 1995, Marino became number one. In that one season, he broke the four major career-passing marks held by former Vikings and Giants quarterback Fran Tarkenton. As each record fell, the games were stopped, and fans, coaches, and players applauded the accomplishments of one of the NFL's best players.

Marino has led the Dolphins to the playoffs seven times, including three trips to the AFC Championship Game. He is also a master of the comeback, leading Miami from behind thirty-two times in the fourth quarter in his career. Off the field, Dan has appeared in movies such as *Ace Ventura: Pet Detective* and was also in a Hootie and the Blowfish music video.

DAN MARINO

MARINO'S MILESTONES

Nine Pro Bowls • 1984, 1986 AFC passing leader • 1983 NFL rookie of
the year • Career Leader (through the 1996 season) in

> Attempts (6,904)
>
> Completions (4,134)
>
> Yards passing (51,636)
>
> Touchdown passes (369)

MARINO BY THE NUMBERS

	Att.	Comp.	TDs	Yards	Ints	Rating
1996	373	221	17	2,795	9	87.8
Career	6,904	4,134	369	51,636	209	88.3

The Dan Marino Foundation

I love throwing touchdown passes. But I also love helping kids. The Dan Marino Foundation helps kids and adults in a variety of programs all over Florida. These programs provide food, clothing, health care, tutoring, and counseling to those in need. Here are some of the ways we raise money for these programs: the Dan Marino FirstPlus Celebrity Invitational (a two-day golf tournament attended by some of my fellow NFL players), Touchdowns for Tots (companies contribute money to this fund every time I throw a touchdown pass), Dan Jam (a benefit concert—last year, Hootie and the Blowfish played), and the Dan Marino Sports Luncheon (fans can help a worthy cause and meet some of my Dolphins teammates). All these events help raise money for dozens of agencies and programs that need help to do their good work.

My family and I are pleased and proud that we can help make so many kids' lives better. If you'd like to help, too, write the Dan Marino Foundation, 1304 SW 160th Ave., Suite 205, Sunrise, FL 33326.

Thank you!
Go Dolphins!

Score an NFL Fan Packet today!

NFL

Get the scoop on all your favorite players with your own NFL Fan Packet! Filled with the hot inside info you can't get anywhere else, this exclusive packet includes the NFL's Play Football Calendar, plus lots of great extras.

For your free NFL Fan Packet, send your name and address and favorite team name to the following address:

NFL Fan Packet
Starline Sports Marketing
1480 Terrell Rd., Marietta, GA 30067

Get off the sidelines and onto the field with NFL.COM

PLAY FOOTBALL

abc MONDAY NIGHT FOOTBALL CLUB

NFL.COM is the official website of the National Football league and the ultimate on-line destination for football fans. From late-breaking news to comprehensive team profiles to live scores and play-by-play every Game Day, NFL.COM covers it all. Fans can interact with their favorite players, sound off in polls and chat about the "big game." And beginning with the 1997 season, a brand new section devoted to kids—Play Football!—will make its debut. Filled with fun games, stats, and trivia, the Play Football! area will be hot! Check it out.

Check out NFL.COM for links to the Monday Night Football Club to find out which football star the guys will switch with next!

Suit up for the big game in official NFL gear

NFL YOUTH PROGRAMS

NFL Flag presented by Nike

Get into flag football competition with the NFL Flag program.
Competitive leagues and instruction are divided into appropriate age
groups for boys and girls age 6–14.
Leagues take place in the fall and spring in Arizona, Carolina,
Chicago, Cincinnati, Cleveland, Dallas, Denver, Jacksonville, Kansas City,
Miami, New England, Philadelphia, and San Diego.

For information on how to get involved, call 1-800-NFL-SNAP

Gatorade NFL Punt, Pass & Kick
September 1997

How far can you throw a football? Can you connect with your receiver?
How far can you kick it? Can you send it sailing through the
middle of the goal post? Show off your football talents at the country's
largest skills competition for boys and girls ages 8–15.

For more information on the competition nearest you, call 1-800-NFL-SNAP

NFL C.I.T.Y. FOOTBALL

Play Football—NFL C.I.T.Y. Football offers boys and girls ages 6-11 from
"at risk" communities, an opportunity to participate in football throughout
the year in Chicago, Detroit, New Orleans, New York, and Oakland, free
of charge. Learn the game through the following programs: Summer Day
Camps, Fall Flag League, and Punt, Pass, & Kick. For more information
on how to join or become involved, please call the following numbers:

New York & Detroit: (516) 844-1823
Chicago: (312) 567-7758 or (312) 280 3000
Oackland: (510) 238-3494
New Orleans: (504) 826-1775

Kmart NFL Family Days

Boys and Girls ages 8–15, listen up and win! Three hundred lucky families
of four in each of the cities below will have the chance to get on the field
and go behind the scenes with Kmart NFL Family Days. Go right into
your local stadium for a day of interactive clinics, coaches chats, insider
tours and more. Camps take place in Carolina, Dallas, Detroit,
Jacksonville, New York (Jets), Oakland, and Washington
during weeks 3–10 of the NFL season.

For registration information, contact your local Kmart.

Enter the NFL/Monday Night Football Club Fantasy Sweepstakes

What's your football fantasy?

Tell us your story and turn fantasy into reality.

- Being the receiver to John Elway's quarterback?
- Passing to Barry Sanders AND escaping the sack?
- Calling the plays in a Super Bowl huddle?
- Getting drafted by your favorite pro NFL team?

Grand Prize:

An all-expense-paid trip to the Footaction NFL Quarterback Challenge for a chance to see your favorite NFL football players in action!

Here's the Game Plan:

- Tell us your football fantasy in 200 words or less (printed or typed).
- Attach a 3x5 card with your name, address, city, state, zip code, and birthdate to the upper right corner of the first page of your story.
- Mail to NFL/Monday Night Football Club Fantasy Sweepstakes, 114 Fifth Avenue, New York, NY 10011.
- Make sure your entry is postmarked no later that February 2, 1998.
- You must be at least 7 years old but not older than 14 by February 2, 1998 to enter.

Hot Hint On How To Score: Give your fantasy a reality check— incorporate real players and places into your story!

FOOTBALL CLUB FANTASY SWEEPSTAKES OFFICIAL RULES

NO PURCHASE NECESSARY

ENTER: Handprint full name and address (city, state or province and zip or mail code), daytime phone with area code and birthdate on a 3" x 5" card; on a separate sheet of paper write an original story about a football fantasy no longer than 200 words; staple the card to the upper right corner of the first page of the story and mail it, postage prepaid, to NFL/Monday Night Football Club Fantasy Sweepstakes, 114 Fifth Avenue, New York, NY 10011, postmarked by February 2, and received by February 6, 1998.

2. ENTRY LIMITATIONS: Limit one entry per person. Story must be an original work and hand printed or typed. Entries which meet all the requirements will be eligible for the sweepstakes drawing. Open only to children between 7 and 14 upon entering who are legal residents of the U.S.A. (excluding its territories, possessions, overseas military installations and commonwealths) or Canada (excluding Quebec) and not employees of Disney Publishing, (the "Sponsor"), The National Football League, their parent, subsidiary or affiliated companies, the advertising, promotional or fulfillment agencies of any of them, nor members of their immediate families. Sponsor is not responsible for printing errors or inaccurate, incomplete, stolen, lost, illegible, mutilated, postage-due, misdirected, delayed or late entries or mail, or equipment or telephone malfunction.

3. RESERVATIONS: Void where prohibited or restricted by law and subject to all federal, state, provincial and local laws and regulations. All entries become the Sponsor's property and will not be returned. By entering this sweepstakes, each entrant agrees to be bound by these rules and the decisions of the judges. Acceptance of prize constitutes the grant of an unconditional right to use winner's name, picture, voice and/or likeness for any and all publicity, advertising and promotional purposes without additional compensation, except where prohibited by law. Sponsor is not responsible for claims, injuries, losses or damages of any kind resulting from the acceptance, use, misuse, possession, loss or misdirection of the prize.

4.WINNER: Will be notified by mail after February 14, 1997. Prize will be awarded in the name of the parent/legal guardian of the winner. Winner is required to prove eligibility. The failure of a potential winner's parent/legal guardian to verify address and execute and return an Affidavit of Eligibility/Release within ten (10) days from the date of notification, or the return of a notification as undeliverable, will result in disqualification and the selection of an alternate winner. All travelers will be required to execute a Release of Liability prior to ticketing. A Canadian resident who is a winner will be required to correctly answer a mathematical skills test to be eligible to collect the prize. For the name of winner (after February 14, 1998) and/or sweepstakes rules, send a self-addressed, stamped envelope to NFL/Monday Night Football Club Fantasy Sweepstakes, 114 Fifth Avenue, New York, NY 10011. WA and VT residents may omit the return postage.

5.PROCEDURES: Sweepstakes begins on September 15, 1997, and ends on February 2, 1998. Winner will be selected from all eligible entries received in a random drawing on or about February 14, 1998, under the supervision of the Marketing Division of Hyperion Books for Children as judges. Odds of winning depend on the number of eligible entries received.

6.PRIZE: One (1) GRAND PRIZE: A four (4) days/three(3) nights trip for four (4) to the 1998 NFL Quarterback Challenge (the "Event"). The date and location of the Event is yet to be determined by The National Football League. The trip includes VIP seating in players' hospitality area for one (1) day at the Event, coach air transportation to/from the major metropolitan airport nearest to winner's home and the major airport nearest the Event, airport transfers and hotel accommodations (one room) for three (3) nights in the city of the Event. All taxes and expenses not mentioned herein are not included and are the responsibility of the winner. Winner must be willing to make the trip during the Event, or an alternate winner will be selected. (Approximate retail value of trip: $2,000.) Prize is not redeemable for cash or transferable and no substitution allowed except at the sole discretion of the Sponsor, who may substitute a prize of equal or greater value if the Event is cancelled for any reason. The prize will be awarded. NFL Films, Inc., NFL Properties, Inc., NFL Enterprises, L.P., the NFL, its member professional football teams ("Member Clubs") and each of their respective affiliates, officers, directors, agents, and employees (collectively, "the NFL") will have no liability or responsibility for any claim arising in connection with participation in this sweepstakes or offer or any prize awarded. The NFL has not offered or sponsored this sweepstakes in any way.